BBC CHILDREN'S BOOKS

Published by the Penguin Group
Penguin Books Ltd, 80 Strand, London WC2R 0RL, England
Penguin Group (USA) Inc., 375 Hudson Street, New York, New York 10014, USA
Penguin Group (Canada), 90 Eglinton Avenue East, Suite 700, Toronto, Ontario, Canada M4P 2Y3
(a division of Pearson Penguin Canada Inc.)
Penguin Ireland, 25 St Stephen's Green, Dublin 2, Ireland (a division of Penguin Books Ltd)
Penguin Group (Australia), 707 Collins Street, Melbourne, Victoria 3008, Australia
(a division of Pearson Australia Group Pty Ltd)
Penguin Books India Pvt Ltd, 11 Community Centre, Panchsheel Park, New Delhi – 110 017, India
Penguin Group (NZ), 67 Apollo Drive, Rosedale, Auckland 0632, New Zealand
(a division of Pearson New Zealand Ltd)
Penguin Books (South Africa) (Pty) Ltd, Block D, Rosebank Office Park,
181 Jan Smuts Avenue, Parktown North, Gauteng 2193, South Africa
Penguin Books Ltd, Registered Offices: 80 Strand, London WC2R 0RL, England

puffinbooks.com

© BBC Children's Books, 2014
Written by Moray Laing
Comic illustrations by John Ross
Comic colours by James Offredi
Short story illustration by Lee Sullivan
001

BBC, DOCTOR WHO (word marks, logos and devices), TARDIS, DALEKS, CYBERMAN and K-9 (word marks
and devices) are trademarks of the British Broadcasting Corporation and are used under licence.
BBC logo © BBC, 1996. Doctor Who logo © BBC, 2014. Dalek image © BBC/Terry Nation 1963.
Cyberman image © BBC/Kit Pedler/Gerry Davis 1966. K-9 image © BBC/Bob Baker/Dave Martin 1977.

Licensed by BBC Worldwide Limited
All rights reserved

Printed in Italy

ISBN: 978–1–405–91756–8

contents

MEET THE NEW DOCTOR!

The Doctor has regenerated . . .

It all happened very quickly. One moment Clara was talking to her best friend – the man who had shown her some of the most amazing sights in the universe – and the next thing she knew, she was staring at a completely different face.

DOCTOR . . . WHO?

- The Doctor is over two thousand years old.
- He's a Time Lord from the planet Gallifrey.
- He can change his whole appearance if his body becomes old or damaged. And it's happened again!

This new Doctor looks older and wiser. He doesn't wear bow ties any more. He's alien and unpredictable – he might be laughing and joking one minute but he will be deadly serious seconds later. He can be your best friend or, if you're a Dalek, your worst enemy. And his home is a massive time-travelling TARDIS disguised as a small police box.

CLARA

The Doctor is often joined on his travels by Clara Oswald, an English teacher at London's Coal Hill School. She has an incredible life that she likes to keep quiet about. After all, who would believe her if she told anyone about her adventures in time and space?

TARDIS MISSION

Bits of the Doctor's TARDIS are scattered throughout this book. Write down the page you find each part on here to put the time machine back together again.

1. ☐
2. ☐
3. ☐
4. ☐
5. ☐
6. ☐

POLICE

POLICE TELEPHONE
FREE
FOR USE OF
PUBLIC
ADVICE & ASSISTANCE
OBTAINABLE IMMEDIATELY
OFFICERS & CARS
RESPOND TO ALL CALLS
PULL TO OPEN

THE DOCTOR'S DIARY

The Doctor's life is full of danger and fun. And very occasionally, he gets the chance to write it down . . .

IMPOSSIBLE CLARA

I don't know what I would do without Clara. She's SAVED MY LIFE more times than I can remember – which is only fair, because I save her life a lot, too! Initially I couldn't figure out why I kept meeting a girl who looked like her in different times and places. Turned out Clara had jumped into my time-stream to save me from the GREAT INTELLIGENCE. Different versions of her were scattered

THROUGHOUT TIME.

* * *

THE TIME WAR

While I was rescuing Clara from my time-stream, I was forced to remember a secret from my past – a big, old secret from the dark days of the Time War. There was a version of me who fought in the Time War. One I try to forget. But together we formed a gang of Doctors and we defeated the DALEKS! We were able to save my home planet Gallifrey, too.

TRENZALORE

I ended up living on Trenzalore for a few centuries. Funny place, but the people are friendly enough. I protected it from countless monster invasions. Eventually I'd reached the end of my life, all regenerated out . . . but Clara begged the **TIME LORDS** to help me and they sent me a whole new **REGENERATION CYCLE** just in time.

ALL CHANGE!

So that's how I got this face. It's different, but I think it works. Though I'm still getting used to the _eyebrows_. Clara looked shocked to begin with, but then she would, wouldn't she? I spent my first few hours riding round the streets of Victorian London in a NIGHTSHIRT trying to stop some rubbish robots from the dawn of time. I feel bad about the dinosaur I brought with me, though . . .

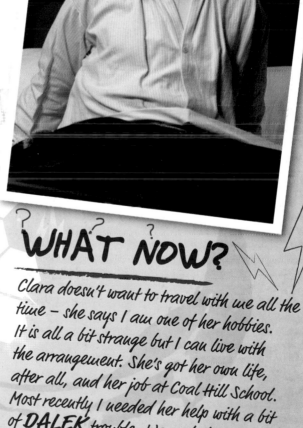

WHAT NOW?

Clara doesn't want to travel with me all the time – she says I am one of her hobbies. It is all a bit strange but I can live with the arrangement. She's got her own life, after all, and her job at Coal Hill School. Most recently I needed her help with a bit of **DALEK** trouble. We ended up inside one. **LONG STORY!**

DOCTOR

You've met the latest Doctor, but what about all the others? Read on to discover the essential facts!

THE FIRST DOCTOR
Played by William Hartnell (1963–1966)
First regular appearance:
An Unearthly Child
Last regular appearance:
The Tenth Planet
Character: Strict, occasionally grumpy
Most likely to say: 'Mmmm?'

THE THIRD DOCTOR
Played by Jon Pertwee (1970–1974)
First regular appearance:
Spearhead from Space
Last regular appearance: *Planet of the Spiders*
Character: Quick-tempered,
gadget-loving scientist
Most likely to say: 'I've reversed the polarity…'

THE FIFTH DOCTOR
Played by Peter Davison (1981–1984)
First regular appearance: *Castrovalva*
Last regular appearance:
The Caves of Androzani
Character: Young, sporty,
Edwardian gentleman
Most likely to say: 'Brave heart…'

THE SECOND DOCTOR
Played by Patrick Troughton (1966–1969)
First regular appearance:
The Power of the Daleks
Last regular appearance: *The War Games*
Character: Fun, full of mischief
Most likely to say:
'When I say run, run!'

THE FOURTH DOCTOR
Played by Tom Baker (1974–1981)
First regular appearance: *Robot*
Last regular appearance: *Logopolis*
Character: Friendly, alien,
short-tempered, kind
Most likely to say: 'Would you like a
jelly baby?'

THE SIXTH DOCTOR
Played by Colin Baker (1984–1986)
First regular appearance:
The Twin Dilemma
Last regular appearance:
The Trial of a Time Lord
Character: Grumpy, over the top, loud
Most likely to say: 'What?!'

WHO?

THE SEVENTH DOCTOR
Played by Sylvester McCoy (1987–1996)
First regular appearance:
Time and the Rani
Last regular appearance: *Survival*
Character: Child-like, mysterious, funny
Most likely to say: 'Will you stop asking me these questions?'

THE WAR DOCTOR
Played by John Hurt (2013)
First regular appearance:
The Name of the Doctor
Last regular appearance:
The Day of the Doctor
Most likely to say: 'I won't remember all this, will I?'

THE TENTH DOCTOR
Played by David Tennant (2005–2010)
First regular appearance:
The Christmas Invasion
Last regular appearance:
The End of Time
Character: Fun, energetic, cheeky
Most likely to say: 'Allons-y!'

THE EIGHTH DOCTOR
Played by Paul McGann (1996 and 2013)
First appearance:
Doctor Who – The Movie
Last appearance:
The Night of the Doctor
Character: Enthusiastic Edwardian gentleman
Most likely to say: 'No-no-no-no!'

THE NINTH DOCTOR
Played by Christopher Eccleston (2005)
First regular appearance: *Rose*
Last regular appearance:
The Parting of the Ways
Character: Thoughtful, emotional, fun
Most likely to say: 'Fantastic!'

THE ELEVENTH DOCTOR
Played by Matt Smith (2010–2013)
First regular appearance:
The Eleventh Hour
Last regular appearance:
The Time of the Doctor
Character: Puppyish, clumsy, determined
Most likely to say: 'Geronimo!'

REGENERAT

Why has the Doctor had so many faces? It's because he is able to regenerate . . .

Time Lords have a very special and useful power – it's called regeneration. If their body becomes too old or is damaged, the process kicks in and every cell in his or her body will change.

A Time Lord can regenerate fully twelve times, meaning in their lifetime they will have thirteen different bodies. Luckily for the Doctor, when he used up all his regenerations he was given a whole new life cycle by the Time Lords.

THE DOCTOR'S LIFE SO FAR . . .

The **First Doctor** regenerated because his body was old and frail.

The **Second Doctor** was forced to regenerate as punishment by the Time Lords.

The **Third Doctor's** body was damaged by radiation on the planet Metebelis III.

The **Fourth Doctor** fell from a great height after saving the universe.

The **Fifth Doctor** was infected and poisoned on Androzani Minor.

The **War Doctor's** body was old after fighting in the Time War.

The **Ninth Doctor** changed after he saved his companion Rose by absorbing the Time Vortex.

The **Eighth Doctor** regenerated during the Time War with help from the Sisterhood of Karn.

The **Tenth Doctor** used up a regeneration after he was blasted by a Dalek. And then later, like the Third, he was damaged by a massive dose of radiation.

The **Seventh Doctor** was shot when he walked out of the TARDIS into gunfire.

The **Sixth Doctor** regenerated after the TARDIS was forced to land with a bump on the planet Lakertya.

So, although he called himself the **Eleventh Doctor,** this Doctor was actually the twelfth incarnation of the Time Lord. His body was old and the Time Lords saved him just before he died.

WHERE'S THE DOCTOR?

Can you spot all thirteen Doctors in this scene?
Tick the boxes when you find them!

- ☒ First Doctor
- ☒ Second Doctor
- ☒ Third Doctor
- ☒ Fourth Doctor
- ☒ Fifth Doctor
- ☒ Sixth Doctor
- ☒ Seventh Doctor
- ☒ Eighth Doctor
- ☒ War Doctor
- ☒ Ninth Doctor
- ☒ Tenth Doctor
- ☒ Eleventh Doctor
- ☒ Twelfth Doctor

THE DALEKS

Things to look out for if you are nano-shrunk and end up inside a Dalek . . .

WHO ARE THEY?

The Daleks are one of the most evil races in the universe. They don't like anything other than their own kind – and they are one of the Doctor's oldest and most cunning enemies.

WHAT IS NANO-SHRINKING?

This is clever technology that allows humans to be shrunk in size. The Doctor and Clara are nano-scaled so they can be dropped inside a damaged Dalek.

EYE STALK
The most vulnerable external part of the Dalek.

CORTEX VAULT
This is what keeps the Dalek pure and full of hatred – a supplementary electronic brain with memory banks.

SENSORS
Dalek sensors can pick up the slightest noise.

POWER LINES
Lead to the trionic fuel cell.

5 SCARIEST DALEK MOMENTS!

1 Discovering that Oswin Oswald was actually a Dalek.

2 Rory realising he's surrounded by crazy Daleks in the Asylum.

3 Breaking free from chains with the help of the Doctor's companion, Rose Tyler.

4 Helping Davros steal Earth and place it in another part of the galaxy.

5 Their first appearance on television – they glided into view and were an instant hit!

LIVING CREATURE
Inside each Dalekanium tank is a yucky mutant creature with a single eye.

ARMOUR CASING
Made from almost indestructible Dalekanium.

EXTERMINATE!

BLASTER
Deadly weapon. Daleks calibrate their blasters to the exact mass of their victims.

DALEK FOOD PLANT
Daleks need protein, and they occasionally harvest it from their victims. There is a big feeding tube inside the Daleks – and it's the weakest spot in its internal security.

KNOW YOUR BOTS!

DROIDS AND THE HALF-FACE MAN

When the SS *Marie Antoinette*, a fifty-first century time-travelling spaceship, crashes in the past, repair droids try to patch up their ship using human body parts. The Half-Face Man is the main control node – pieced together from human remains.

K-9

Long before Handles, the Doctor had another robot friend – this one looked like a dog and was called K-9. There are several versions of this clever and loyal robot dog. One of them looked after the Doctor's former companion, Sarah Jane Smith, on Earth.

CYBERMEN

Cybermen used to be human, but they replaced their limbs with mechanical parts. The only remaining trace of the human body inside is the brain. Cyber technology came up with an emotional inhibitor to remove any emotions from the poor creature remaining inside the suit.

Mechanical Men

SPOONHEADS

The Doctor says they are walking Wi-Fi base stations that hoover people up. These robots are used by the Great Intelligence to load people up in to a data cloud. They can shape-shift into human replicas. The Doctor rewires one to drive up the Shard and break into the Great Intelligence's HQ.

HANDLES

This friendly robot head travelled with the Doctor in the TARDIS for a while. The Doctor got him cheaply in the Maldovar market. The organic insides are all gone, but there is a complete set of data-banks inside this little Cyberhead.

GADGET

The crew of Bowie Base One on Mars have a robot called Gadget. It says 'Gadget Gadget!' when it understands a command. When terrifying water monsters called the Flood take over the Base, Gadget saves the Doctor and some of the crew by fetching the TARDIS.

TARDIS TROUBLE

A dangerous time storm is affecting the TARDIS. Look at the pictures closely to work out which is the correct one.

1

2

3

4

5

6

7

8

22

Secret Cyber Code

Handles has left a secret message for the Doctor using pictures of his old enemies. Use the code at the bottom of the page to work out what the message says!

Hurry! The

cybermen Have

captured clara!

sHe Needs you!

Help Now!

A B C D E F G H I J K L M

N O P Q R S T U V W X Y Z

I LIKE A GANG!

THE PATERNOSTER GANG

Meet the world's most unusual group of detectives!

WHO ARE THEY?

In nineteenth century London, three friends form a secret group that becomes known as the Paternoster Gang. They solve crimes for Scotland Yard and live at 13 Paternoster Row. The group consists of Silurian Madame Vastra, her wife and maid, Jenny Flint, and Strax the Sontaran butler.

HELPING THE DOCTOR

Vastra, Jenny and Strax play a big part in helping the Doctor to start travelling in time and space again. After helping him defeat the Great Intelligence and an army of carnivorous snowmen, the Doctor sets off in the TARDIS determined to solve the mystery of Clara's identity.

THE CRIMSON HORROR

The Doctor meets the gang again when they rescue him from Sweetville and help him uncover the strange things happening there. A nasty old woman called Mrs Gillyflower has a horrible plan to destroy Earth with an alien poison – but is stopped by the gang, along with the Doctor and Clara.

STRAX

VASTRA

JENNY

TRENZALORE TRIP

Jenny is killed by the mysterious Whisper Men and Strax and Vastra are taken to Trenzalore by the Great Intelligence. On the planet, time alters and they forget they are friends, which leads to Vastra killing the Sontaran. Luckily, Clara was able to fix time and this brought them all back to life.

DINO DANGER

The newly regenerated Twelfth Doctor and Clara run into the gang again soon after he accidentally brings a dinosaur to Victorian London. Together they fight the dangerous Half-Face Man and his almost unstoppable droids.

Where do you think the Doctor will meet the Paternoster Gang next?

Write your answer here:

31

LOOK OUT!

There are ten differences in these two pictures. Can you find them all?

DID YOU JUST SEE SOMETHING STRANGE?

THE SILENCE

Don't take your eyes off these silent scarers!

SCREAM TEAM

These tall dome-headed monsters are horrific to look at and straight out of your worst nightmare! They can fire electricity from their hands that can kill you instantly. And the strange thing is, as soon as you look away from them you'll forget you ever saw one . . .

REBEL PRIESTS

Silents are alien priests in the Church of the Papal Mainframe. A renegade group, known as the Kovarian Chapter, travelled back along the Doctor's timeline. They wanted to stop him ever reaching the planet Trenzalore, where a new Time War would begin if the Doctor reveals his true name.

KIDNAP!

The rebel group of Silents steal Amy and Rory's daughter. They turn her against the Doctor and send her on a mission to kill him. Years later, she falls in love with the Time Lord and even marries him. Her name is River Song!

CRACKS IN TIME

The Silents are also responsible for blowing up the Doctor's TARDIS and creating huge cracks through time. This isn't caused, as the Doctor jokingly says, because he left the bath running . . .

SILENT DALEKS

During the Siege of Trenzalore, the Daleks take control of the Papal Mainframe. Dalek nanogenes affect the Silents, along with everyone else, turning them into sinister Dalek puppets.

WHEN THE
WOLVES CAME

The howling and snarling was terrifying. Simon stopped for only a brief moment to catch his breath, knowing that he had to be quick. The wolves were now following his scent and they were close.

The young boy was scared. This struggle to survive wasn't new to him but he hadn't seen any other survivors for a couple of months now. Worse still, he was running out of places to find food. This time he had only managed to track down a tin of baked beans.

London towards the end of the twenty-second century was a dark and dangerous place. Devastated after an alien invasion, there was now rubble where impressive buildings had once stood. One day, the wolves came. No one knew where from. Hungry, wild and out of control, they took over the city. London belonged to them now.

The whole city was considered unstable and dangerous. The army eventually decided to move people out, but some people, like Simon, got left behind . . .

Right, he thought. Time to move. Sprinting at full speed, rain soaked his skin as he ran through the empty streets. Without warning, he slipped and fell flat on his face. The tin he was carrying flew out of his hands and rolled down the hill.

He got up as fast as he could. The first things he saw were two wolves watching him from the other side of the road, their eyes glinting menacingly.

Running for his life, he turned the corner and there it was – the strange blue police box that had kept him safe all these months . . .

Simon dashed towards the box. As he reached the door, it opened inwards by itself, allowing him to enter. It slammed shut behind him as the two wolves crashed head first into the closed door. They howled angrily.

Simon was lying on the cold floor, exhausted and hungry. His dangerous journey had been a failure and he had returned to his base without food. But at least he was safe.

The confusing thing about the box was that it was much bigger on the inside than it should have been. As his eyes adjusted to the dim light, he looked around the large room. The boy stumbled around lighting some candles and wondered what he was going to do. What if the wolves stayed outside the box and kept him trapped in here forever? He'd starve!

Simon walked up to the controls and touched one of the many panels. 'Please help me,' he heard himself saying out loud. 'Please, I'm desperate!'

The panel glowed blue, then, one by one, lights lit up around the room. Everything started to shake and then there was a noise unlike any noise Simon had heard before. What was happening?

He watched as a tall man and a girl slowly appeared out of nowhere. Ghostly blue figures at first, they soon became solid and real. They looked surprised. The man spoke first.

'About time, too! I'm sure that you've got no idea what you've done,' said the man.

'What he means is thank you,' said the girl. 'You've just saved our bacon.'

'The TARDIS brought you to us,' the tall man continued. 'She's clearly been looking after you while she's been stuck in the twenty-second century. Seems we all needed help at the same time, though, and you must have triggered something in the telepathic circuits! You materialised around us just as we were about to be turned into toast by an Aaraandandal slime beast. Very nasty.'

Simon started speaking and found he couldn't stop. These were the first people he had spoken to in a very long time. They listened as he told them about being left behind in London, the wolves, and finding the baffling blue box. The girl smiled at him kindly.

'We can take you somewhere far safer than London,' announced the man. 'Hold on tight!' Simon heard the strange sound again, the room shook and moments later the three of them were stepping outside the box into a room with two people Simon recognised immediately – his mum and dad. Stunned, the three of them hugged each other tightly.

'Where are we?' asked Simon.

'I've moved you to outside the danger zone – a bit north of London,' replied the tall man. 'I think it's called Bedfordshire. You'll be safe here.'

'Thank you!' said Simon, almost unable to believe his luck and suddenly aware the tall man and girl were going back inside the blue box. He raised his hand in farewell, as he watched the box fade away until it was no longer there.

THE ZYGONS

Beware these shape-changing aliens!

WHO ARE THEY?

The monstrous Zygons are orange-skinned creatures with sharp teeth and suckers all over their bodies. They come from the planet Zygor, which was destroyed in the Time War.

POISON

Deadly venom sacs are found in their mouths. They are also able to sting a victim with a single touch.

EARTH INVADERS

The creatures can live for several centuries and have been spotted on Earth many times. The Doctor, Amy and Rory discover that there is a Zygon spaceship underneath a hotel in London – and half the staff are shape-shifters! Some Zygons also join a monster alliance against the Doctor at Stonehenge.

THE LOCH NESS MONSTER

After their world is destroyed, a Zygon spaceship crashes into Loch Ness in Scotland. They have a massive pet called a Skarasen, which people mistake for the Loch Ness Monster. The Fourth Doctor defeats them, along with help from his friends Sarah Jane and Harry.

SHAPE-CHANGERS

The Zygons are able to blend in on Earth because they are able to change their shape – they can easily transform into any living creature. To do this, they must keep the person they are copying alive, though.

HIDING

Because they like the look of Earth as a new planet but didn't like the time period they had arrived in, a group of them decide to hide inside special 3D paintings. They wait a few centuries until the planet is a bit more interesting, and then invade.

PEACE TALKS

On Earth in 2013, the Zygons and their human copies became trapped inside UNIT's Black Archive by three versions of the Doctor. They talk for a long time until they finally find a peaceful solution.

THE SONTARANS

Essential facts about a spud-headed race of clones!

SURRENDER TO THE GLORY OF THE SONTARAN EMPIRE!

WHO ARE THEY?

When it comes to fighting, Sontarans are supreme! These short, squat aliens come from the planet Sontar. When they remove their helmet, the first thing you will notice is an angry face that looks like a furious baked potato. Don't laugh at them though, because the Sontarans are extremely dangerous. They are an old enemy of the Doctor, and he has met them many times.

CLONE WARRIORS

The Sontaran race is bred for just one thing – battle. Large numbers of soldiers can be created at the same time, which is perfect for making an instant army that will fight until they achieve victory or die trying.

DANGEROUS ENEMIES

Sontarans have been at war with an alien race called the Rutans for a long time. Like Zygons, these Rutan creatures have the ability to change shape. They are as ruthless and as brilliant at fighting as the Sontarans – so they have been battling for thousands of years.

WAR CHANT

Listen out for their war cry – Sontarans like to chant 'Sontar-ha!' before going into battle.

WEAK SPOT

Sontarans may possess the best military minds, but they have one fatal flaw. Their one weak spot is a small hole on the back of their necks called a Probic Vent. If something hits this area hard enough, it can kill a Sontaran instantly.

STRAX

There is one Sontaran unlike any other – and he's a good friend of the Doctor's. Strax has helped the Time Lord many times. As a nurse, he was killed during a battle at Demon's Run. Madame Vastra and Jenny then brought him back to life, and he now lives with them as a butler in Victorian England.

HIDDEN HORRORS

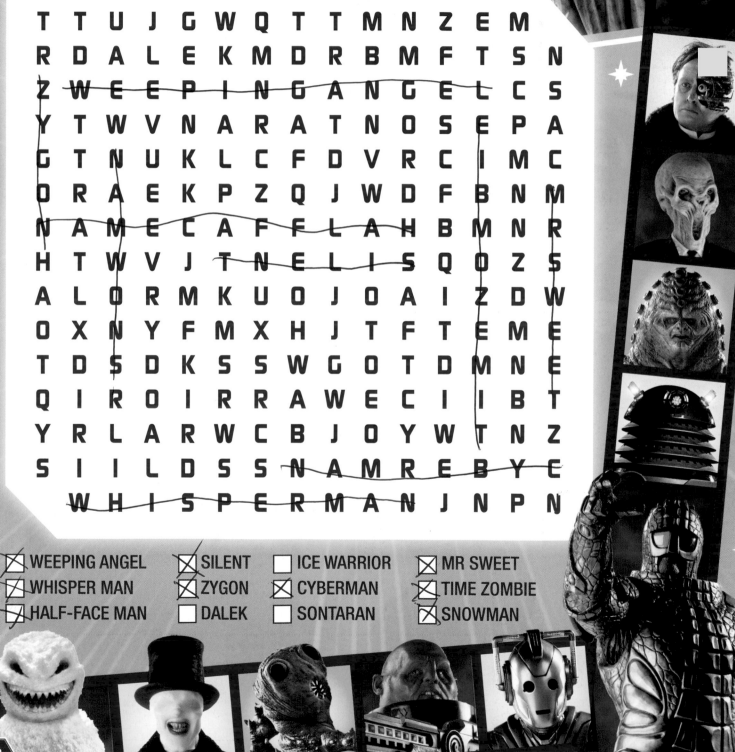

Find and circle the different monsters hiding in this wordsearch. They appear up, down and backwards too!

```
T T U J G W Q T T M N Z E M
R D A L E K M D R B M F T S N
Z W E E P I N G A N G E L C S
Y T W V N A R A T N O S E P A
G T N U K L C F D V R C I M C
O R A E K P Z Q J W D F B N M
N A M E C A F F L A H B M N R
H T W V J T N E L I S Q O Z S
A L O R M K U O J O A I Z D W
O X N Y F M X H J T F T E M E
T D S D K S S W G O T D M N E
Q I R O I R R A W E C I I B T
Y R L A R W C B J O Y W T N Z
S I I L D S S N A M R E B Y C
W H I S P E R M A N J N P N
```

- ☒ WEEPING ANGEL
- ☒ WHISPER MAN
- ☒ HALF-FACE MAN
- ☒ SILENT
- ☒ ZYGON
- ☐ DALEK
- ☐ ICE WARRIOR
- ☒ CYBERMAN
- ☐ SONTARAN
- ☒ MR SWEET
- ☒ TIME ZOMBIE
- ☒ SNOWMAN

42

UNDERGROUND TRAP!

Strax is stuck underground and needs to get back to Vastra and Jenny. Quickly lead him through the maze – and avoid the Half-Face Man and his droids!

HOLD YOUR BREATH IF YOU BUMP INTO A DROID!

FINISH

START

DANGEROUS PLANETS >>

According to the TARDIS files, the following planets are considered dangerous and unsuitable to Earth visitors, so read carefully and if you end up on one of them, make sure you don't hang around there for long.

TRENZALORE

Time travellers beware! There are two very different versions of Trenzalore available to you. Both are dangerous. One is a sleepy planet with a snowy village called Christmas where no one can tell a lie. It gets attacked a lot by monsters! The other is a graveyard world with a large, dead TARDIS and a cemetery full of victims from the Siege of Trenzalore. Whisper Men wander there.

VERDICT: Chance of death – high!

SKARO

This planet is the birthplace of the Daleks – so that information alone should send you running! A long and devastating war between the Kaleds and the Thals left Skaro with high radiation levels – not good for human travellers, since it will make you very ill. Also, the planet will contain Daleks. Daleks tend to not like non-Dalek visitors and will almost certainly exterminate you.

VERDICT: Best avoided.

MARS

In terms of the huge size of the universe, the red planet is relatively near Earth. In the year 2014, humans still haven't visited Mars . . . but that all changes in the future. By the 2050s, a human colony is set up there, but is destroyed by a water virus called the Flood. The planet is also home to a great and noble race called the Ice Warriors.

VERDICT: It's a beautiful colour, but the locals aren't friendly.

AKHATEN

This living planet survives on the souls of the Sunsingers of Akhet. The planet slept for hundreds of years – so if visiting, best to go during that time period. When the planet wakes up, it's bound to be grumpy and will probably want to eat all the planets nearby. Seven worlds orbit Akhaten, all of them sharing a belief that life in the universe originated here.

VERDICT: Choose your timing carefully.

GALLIFREY

Found in the constellation of Kasterborous, this golden planet is home to the Time Lords, the race that first discovered time travel. Officially, people from Earth aren't allowed to go there, although some of the Doctor's Earth friends have ended up there during emergencies. It was once thought that the planet was destroyed during the Time War . . . but the Doctor saved it and placed it in a parallel pocket universe.

VERDICT: Don't go there without the Doctor!

51

DOCTOR WHO QUIZ

Test your *Doctor Who* knowledge with this quiz!

1 Who plays the Twelfth Doctor?
A Peter Davison
B Peter Capaldi
C Matt Smith

2 Who plays Clara Oswald?
A Jenna Coleman
B Hannah Coleman
C Anna Coleman

3 Where is the Doctor originally from?
A Guildford
B Gallifrey
C Skaro

4 What subject does Clara teach?
A French
B Maths
C English

5 What species is Madame Vastra?
A A Sontaran
B A Silurian
C A Cyberman

6 What is Danny the maths teacher's last name?
A Oswald
B White
C Pink

7 Who played the War Doctor in *The Day of the Doctor*?
A John Hurt
B Tom Baker
C William Hartnell

8 What was the name of the Doctor's Cyberhead friend?
A Rusty
B Handles
C Fred the Head

9 What planet do Zygons come from?
A Zyonia
B Zy
C Zygor

10 What does the R in TARDIS stand for?
A Real
B Relative
C Royal

11 What must you not do if you see a Weeping Angel?
A Blink
B Drink
C Breathe

12 The Doctor used to travel with a robot dog called . . .
A Barker
B Handles
C K-9

13 Who are the Paternoster Gang?
A Madame Vastra, Jenny Flint and Strax
B The Doctor, Clara and Handles
C The Doctor, River Song and the Ponds

14 What is the only remaining human part of a Cyberman?
A The hands
B The brain
C The legs

15 What time-travelling spaceship from the fifty-first century crashed into London?
A SS *Clara Antoinette*
B SS *Marie Antoinette*
C SS *Angela Antoinette*

16 How many times can a Time Lord usually regenerate?
A Six times
B Twelve times
C Twenty times

17 Which creatures are connected to the Kovarian Chapter?
A The Sontarans
B The Silents
C Clockwork droids

18 What is the weak spot of a Sontaran called?
A The cortex vault
B The emotional inhibitor
C The probic vent

19 What did the Twelfth Doctor bring to London by accident on his first TARDIS trip?
A A Dalek
B A dinosaur
C A puppy

20 On what planet would you find a small village called Christmas?
A Skaro
B Earth
C Trenzalore

INSIDE THE DALEK

You're both shrunk down in size and trapped inside a Dalek and there's only one way out – but who will get there first?

HOW TO PLAY

1 Decide who's going to go first and place your counters on the start.

2 Roll the die and move your counter the number shown.

3 Follow any instructions when you land on them.

4 You'll get separated – the winner is the first person to reach the eye stalk.

5 But don't let your friend be trapped inside the Dalek forever – wait for them to reach the end too!

WHAT YOU NEED
A die
Two counters (you can use buttons or coins)
A travelling companion
A sonic screwdriver (if you don't have one, pretend with a pen)

GRAB A FRIEND TO PLAY THIS GAME!

You've done it. Well done!

FINISH

40

39

38

37

36

35

33

32 Use this rope to get ahead to 36.

31

Look out, more Dalek antibodies ahead! Go back five spaces!

34

30 You lose your footing and fall down to 23.

29

28 The tunnel breaks up and you have to jump! So JUMP! Move forward three spaces.

27

26

25 The Dalek asks you for your earliest Dalek

CLARA'S DIARY

WORK!

Teaching English at Coal Hill School is fun. Everyone has been really good to me – although I'm sure they might think I'm a bit strange. (I disappear a lot.) Well, I say a lot – I head off into TIME AND SPACE and am usually back before they've noticed I've gone!

CHRISTMAS

Well, that was probably the weirdest Christmas ever. I panicked (don't know why!) and told my family that I had a boyfriend – called the Doctor. I thought it would make it easier, but it didn't, it really didn't. He turned up at my flat without any clothes on! My poor gran! And making Christmas lunch was REALLY stressful. And then EVERYTHING changed.

THE DOCTOR

I always knew it could happen – because we'd talked about it before. But I don't think I realised HOW different it would be when it actually happened. The Doctor – the mad man I feel like I've known all my life – CHANGED HIS FACE! He looks totally different and has gone all Scottish! But he's still the same brilliant Doctor. I wish he'd put on a bow tie once in a while, though. They were cool.

MY UNUSUAL FRIENDS

I've got some pretty amazing mates these days – and some of them aren't human!
For starters, there's MADAME VASTRA who is a green lizard lady from the dawn of time, and a Sontaran butler called STRAX. They live in the past and we've gone back to see them a few times. Strax isn't the brightest and thinks I'm a young lad. Bless!

DANNY

WOW. Quick update.
DANNY PINK is the new maths teacher. Nice face. Fantastic smile. We're going out for a drink! I'm not sure what he'd make of my life with the Doctor. Better not mention it for a while . . .

MR PINK!

WHERE NOW?

Got to dash. I can hear that magical sound of ancient engines grinding. It means that the Doctor is about to appear and whisk me off on an adventure. I don't think I'll ever get tired of this. Where to this time? CAN'T WAIT to find out. BYE!

TOP ELEVENTH DOCTOR MOMENT!

As the Twelfth Doctor takes control of the TARDIS console in series eight, Top Trumps is challenging you to draw your favourite Eleventh Doctor moment on the blank card below. Scan or photograph your card and send it to the address below, for a chance to win a free pack of Doctor Who Top Trumps and a Turbo game PLUS a chance to be featured on the Top Trumps Facebook page! Address: Eleventh Doctor, Top Trumps Towers, Winning Moves, 7 Praed Street, London W21NJ.

SEASON:

EMOTION:

LAUGHS:

EXCITEMENT & ACTION:

Fill in this card with your favourite moment!

DOCTOR WHO other games available now!

www.toptrumps.co.uk

ANSWERS

TARDIS MISSION

Part 1 of the TARDIS is on p14
Part 2 of the TARDIS is on p9
Part 3 of the TARDIS is on p53
Part 4 of the TARDIS is on p40
Part 5 of the TARDIS is on p35
Part 6 of the TARDIS is on p58

P14–15 WHERE'S THE DOCTOR?

P22 TARDIS TROUBLE

The correct police box is 6

P29 SECRET CYBER CODE

Hurry! The Cybermen have captured Clara!
She needs your help now!

P32–33 SPOT THE DIFFERENCE

P42 HIDDEN HORRORS

P49 UNDERGROUND TRAP

P52–55 DOCTOR WHO QUIZ

1. B (Peter Capaldi)
2. A (Jenna Coleman)
3. B (Gallifrey)
4. C (English)
5. B (A Silurian)
6. C (Pink)
7. A (John Hurt)
8. B (Handles)
9. C (Zygor)
10. B (Relative)
11. A (Blink)
12. C (K-9)
13. A (Madame Vastra, Jenny Flint and Strax)
14. B (The brain)
15. B (SS *Marie Antoinette*)
16. B (twelve times)
17. B (The Silents)
18. C (The probic vent)
19. B (A dinosaur)
20. C (Trenzalore)